Gunfight at Barfield Springs

A Jack Cordell Western

R. Annan

Gunfight at Barfield Springs
Copyright 2015 R. Annan
Edition 1.3
WGA Reg. #: R31459 (6/25/2015)
Printed in the United States of America
Published by One Vision Publishing
e-Book ISBN: 978-1-942338-23-9
Print Book ISBN: 978-1-942338-22-2

Jump into the adventures of Jack Cordell by R. Annan.
The Gunfighter in Winter
Long Ride to Hell's Kitchen
Owl Hawks
Gunfight at Barfield Springs
Shootout at Sanctuary City
Last Days of a Gunfighter (*forthcoming*)

Coming soon: Clay Jared Westerns

Dedicated to

A Brave Soldier and a Patriot

SGM Anthony R. Annan, USA (Retired)

1.

A young cowboy rode into Barfield Springs one Saturday afternoon and stopped at the town stable. He was covered with dust and was very thirsty. He drank deeply at the well there.

"Where kin I get somethin' ta eat," he asked.

"There's a beanery on the other side of town, kid," the stable owner said.

The young man left his horse to be fed, watered, and brushed, and went to find the beanery.

As he approached the front of the Lusty Lady Saloon three Circle D cowboys came out on the porch. The tall lean one, whose name was Lem, carried a bottle of whiskey which he passed around to the other two named Sid and Zeke. Sid was short and Zeke was mid-sized. When they saw the young man they stepped out into the road to block his path.

"Hey kid," Lem said, "have a drink!"

"No thanks," the kid said.

"What, you think yer too good fer us, kid?" Zeke asked.

"Maybe later." The kid smiled and kept walking.

As he went by, Zeke threw a sucker punch at him. The kid saw it coming and ducked. He gave Zeke such a hard shove it sent him back against his two pals.

Lem's hat went sailing out into the road.

He glared at the kid. "Pick it up, you smart son of a bitch!"

The kid ignored him, turned, and continued on up the street.

"Stop, ass hole!" Lem yelled.

"Get back here, kid!" Zeke shouted.

The kid kept walking.

Suddenly there was a gunshot and a bullet kicked up dirt near the heel of the kid's right boot. The young cowboy froze for a second then turned slowly around with his hands up to show he was no threat.

Lem pointed his gun at the kid's belly.

"Come an' pick it up, sonny!" Lem growled threateningly.

"Say please an' I might," the kid said in a calm voice.

The quiet cowboy, Sid, cleared his throat and said, "Forget him Lem! He's just a kid. Let him go. Right, Zeke?"

"Whose side you on, Sid?" Lem growled. "His?"

Sid shrugged and stepped away from Lem and Zeke.

Zeke glared up the street at the lone cowboy.

"He's gonna pick Lem's hat up or I'll bore his dumb ass!" He put the whiskey bottle in his left hand to free his gun hand.

People started to stop and look on, curious as to what was happening, but staying back on the plank sidewalk. Sid, too, put more space between himself and his two belligerent pals.

A few cowboys came out of the Lusty Lady onto the porch to see the action. Most of them were Circle D men.

Lem took up a stance facing the kid. "He's all mine, Zeke," he growled.

Zeke shook his head. "Let's toss for it, Lem. Heads you git ta bore him and tails I git ta do it."

"Come on, guys," Sid said. "He jest a dumb kid! Let it be!"

Lem glanced over at Sid. "You yellow belly coward, Sid! I'm gonna kick yer ass right after I take care of this fool."

"Well, this is murder an' I don't want no part of it," Sid said. He stepped to the side of the road.

"All the stubborn son of a bitch has ta do is pick up Lem's hat," Zeke said. "That's all."

The kid chuckled and said loudly for the crowd to hear, "Hey, ass hole, would an apology make you stop cryin' like a baby about that damn hat?"

"You smart little shit," Lem grumbled. "Yer gonna get it good fer that!

"I'm takin' him!" Zeke yelled. "He's all mine."

"No you ain't! It's my hat!" Lem said.

"Alright, then, go ahead," Zeke conceded. "Drill his ass."

The kid lowered his right hand alongside his holster.

"Somebody best make a move," the kid said. "I'm getting' real hungry."

Lem nodded and moved a few feet away from Zeke and took up the stance, holding his right hand a few inches back and below his holster. He glared intensely at the kid, his fingers twitching nervously.

Suddenly he began the draw. His gun was halfway out when there was a loud blast. Lem's body gave a quick jerk as the kid's bullet hit him in the chest, below the heart, spinning him sideways. He fell forward on the road, dead.

The kid put his Colt back in its holster and waited for Zeke to make his move.

"Yer gonna die, you son of a bitch!" Zeke screamed as he drew.

He got his gun clear and up but never got to pull the trigger. The kid's shot hit him square between the eyes, snapping his head back on his neck. Zeke's body danced crazily for a brief moment. He fired his gun into the ground as his legs turned to rubber and he dropped in a heap on the road.

A few more cowboys came out of the Lusty Lady to see what was going on. One called down from the porch to Sid.

"What happened, Sid?" he asked, a cigarette dangling from the corner of his mouth.

"Lem and Zeke braced that kid. All over a stupid ol' hat, Curt!" Sid whined. "It was fair and square."

"Well, fair or not," Curt said, "the boss won't stand fer it. Nobody plugs a Circle D cowpoke an' gets away with it!"

"But the kid didn't start it, Curt!"

"Don't matter," Curt said confidently. "I gotta fix it right."

Curt stepped down into the road and tossed his cigarette away.

"Where you from, kid?" Curt asked with authority.

"Down around Del Rio," the kid said calmly. "What's it to ya, mister?"

"Well, Del Rio, yer about to meet yer maker. Any last words?"

"Yeah. Kiss my ass."

They both drew. The kid was a second faster. His bullet smacked Curt mid-chest. For a moment he looked surprised then grunted and looked confused. His legs gave out and he sat down in the road.

"You lucky bastard!" Curt groaned, fell back, clutched his chest, and died.

Someone yelled, "The Marshal is comin'!"

An elderly gray-haired man with a Marshal's badge came through the crowd. He was wearing a Colt and carried a double barrel shotgun. He stared at the three bodies. Seconds later he was joined by a middle-aged Deputy.

"Sweet Jesus! What the hell happened here? Someone gonna tell me?" the Marshal asked.

The cowboy called Sid came over. He pointed up at the kid who stood casually thumbing bullets in his Colt.

"They braced the kid, Marshal Phelps," Sid said. "It was a fair fight all the way."

"What was the fight over?"

"A stupid, damn, old hat," Sid said.

"A god-damn hat?" The Marshal couldn't believe it.

One of the Circle D men near Sid said, "Don't come back to the Circle D, Sid. It won't be healthy there fer you anymore, you skunk!"

"Any other witnesses?" the Marshal asked. Three men and a woman raised their hands.

"Alright, you all and you too Sid, come down to the jailhouse and we'll write it all down."

The Marshal turned to his Deputy.

"Dave, go get the buckboard. We gotta get these bodies over to the undertaker."

The Deputy nodded and quickly left. The Marshal walked up to the kid.

"What's yer name, son?"

"Breen, Marshal."

Someone in the crowd yelled, "Breen! Hell, that's Kid Breen! He's from down around Del Rio way!"

"Yeah? So what?" someone in the crowd asked.

"So what? He was mixed up in that cattle an' sheep war down around the Mexican border. He shot six men! That's what!"

"Is that you, son?" Marshal Phelps asked.

The kid shrugged. "Nope. Not me, Marshal. Never been that far south."

"Yer lyin' boy," the Marshal said in a fatherly way.

"Yeah, it's me."

"You got a horse?"

"Yeah, I got a horse."

"Then you best ride outta town," the Marshal said.

"Why? I jest got here, Marshal!"

"And yer just leavin', kid."

"How come?"

"Because you just marked yerself fer death and three bodies is enough for one day. More than enough!" the Marshal said harshly. "Now git outta my town!"

Suddenly a Circle D man stepped into the road.

"He ain't goin' no place, Marshal," the man said. "He's gonna hang here an' now."

The Marshal pointed his shotgun at the man's belly.

"I'm the law in Barfield, not the Circle D," the old Marshal growled. "Now git back inside and mind yer own danged business so I kin take care a mine!" The Marshal looked at the men on the porch. "That goes fer all of you!"

There was some grumbling but they all finally cleared the porch.

"Kid, if you ain't outta my town in ten minutes, I'll arrest you."

The kid shrugged and began walking down to the stable.

"Sid," the Marshal said. "Forget about that statement. You're finished at the Circle D. So you had best go too."

"Yeah, I guess yer right, Marshal."

Sid ran down the road to catch up with the kid.

The owner of the town paper, the Barfield Gazette, came walking up to the scene. When he saw the three bodies he whistled in wonder.

"Wow! What the heck happened, Marshal Phelps?"

"Kid Breen just breezed through town, Earl. When I git this mess cleaned up I'll let you look through the witness reports. It should make a good front page story."

2.

Jack Cordell came over a hill and stopped to look down at the town of Barfield Springs. His horse was tired and so was he. A good feeding, watering, and a rubdown for his mount and a hot meal and bath for him waited below.

Danger could also be waiting there.

Ever since he killed the notorious fast draw Red Hardy, he had been challenged by every kind of crazy gunslinger imaginable. And so far it ended badly for the fools who braced him. So far, that is. That could change in a split second at any time and he could end up dead.

Jack Cordell's life was a game of Russian roulette. And it sometimes scared even him.

Still, he couldn't go on living on the run, jumping at every sound behind him. He'd just have to face it all as it came at him, one day at a time, and hope for the best.

Cordell nudged his horse down the slope. He came in on the south side. The stable was there, just where he figured it would be.

"Treat him to a big bag of yer best oats and a rubdown," Cordell said as he dismounted. "And let him drink. He's pretty thirsty." The stable owner nodded. Cordell tossed him a double eagle in advance. "You'll get another when I come back in the morning, friend."

Cordell left his shaving kit in his saddlebag. He was letting his hair and beard grow. It was the only disguise he had, and even it didn't work every time.

"They got a beanery, mister?" Cordell asked.

"Up past the Lusty Lady Saloon," the man said. "You're a gambler, I see." It was the suit, always the suit.

"You guessed it, friend," Cordell chuckled.

"Be careful. There was some trouble last Saturday. Some kid shot up the town. Things get wild on a Saturday."

"I take it this is a cow town, then?"

"Yep."

Cordell knew what that meant. There would be lots of drinking and gambling going on. With his skill at cards he would probably leave town in the morning with a few hundred more than he came in with. And if he was real lucky he wouldn't have to kill anyone.

Cordell walked slowly north, staying on the plank sidewalk, in the shadows. He soon saw the Lusty Lady up ahead, on the other side. Several cowboys were standing on the porch while several more sat on the railing watching the ladies go by.

A cowboy named Carl spotted Cordell. It was the suit again. He didn't look like a cowboy in a cowboy's town.

"Hey! Carpetbagger!" Carl yelled "Whatcha sellin'? Women's underwear?"

Another cowboy named Jim also took interest in the baiting. It was great sport. "I bet he's a sellin' men's girdles! Haw!"

"Naw! I bet he's a Bible thumper," Carl said, "or he's a sellin' them Farmer's Almanacs."

"Let's have a little fun Carl," Jim said. "Let's see ifn he kin dance."

"Yeah," his buddy said. "I bet he kin do the jig real purdy."

The other cowboys watched as Jim and Carl stepped off the porch and walked over to Cordell. They stood in front of him so that he and the other people had to either stop walking or go around them.

A woman with a child came up beside Cordell.

"Let us pass, please," she said.

Cordell tipped his hat to the lady and moved out into the road. The two cowboys followed, step-by-step, staying in front of him.

"I hear tell a carpetbagger kin dance real purdy," Carl said. "Is thet true?"

"Look, friend," Cordell said. "How about I buy you and your friend here a bottle?" He took a double eagle from his pocket and offered it to Carl.

"How about you jest do a jig fer my pal an' me and we all go get a drink," Jim said. "How about thet, mister carpetbagger?"

"Ah, I'm not a carpetbagger, friend, I'm a gambler."

"Oh, gosh! A gambler," Carl said. "I'm real impressed with thet, mister.

Jim, however, backed off a bit. Some card players were known to be good with a gun, and he knew that. He looked around at the crowd that gathered on the walkway. A few cowboys came up from the Lusty Lady to see the show and urge their pals on. They were expecting action of some sort but Jim suddenly didn't feel up to it.

"Hell," Jim said. "This ain't no fun. Let's forget it, Carl."

"Hell, no, Jim," Carl chuckled. "He's gonna dance us a jig an' thet's thet, ol' buddy!"

"Your friend is talking sense, Carl," Cordell said. "I'm buying the drinks."

"You ain't buyin' shit," Carl sneered and drew his gun.

He didn't get very far. Cordell pulled his Colt and slammed it hard against Carl's head. He dropped like a sack of potatoes.

Cordell holstered his gun and continued walking up the street.

"Hold it!"

Cordell turned. A cowboy stood in the road facing him, his arms down alongside his twin Colts. Cordell stared hard, trying to remember if he'd seen him before. He hadn't.

"Don't do it," Cordell said, almost sadly.

"Why not?"

"You'll die," Cordell said with a sigh.

The cowboy chuckled and drew.

Cordell drew and fired from a crouch. His shot hit the gunslinger in the center of his forehead. His eyes turned up in his head and closed. He dropped down on his knees and fell on his face in the dirt. The other cowboys seemed to know him and gathered around him. One knelt down to see if he was dead.

"Who was he?" Cordell asked.

"He's Elroy Turk," someone in the crowd said. "He's one of the fasted draws on the Circle D. You'd better run, mister. Del Oldring will be comin' after ya."

"Who is Oldring?"

"You'll find out if ya stay around here, friend."

Cordell only shrugged.

"Tell the Marshal I'll be in the beanery," Cordell said as he reloaded his Colt.

An hour later he was in jail.

3.

Marshal Phelps put Jack Cordell in jail for thirty days.

"It's for yer own good," the Marshal said. "I'm doin' you a favor."

"Thanks, Marshal," Cordell chuckled but he didn't see the logic in it.

"You play cards?" the Marshal asked.

"A little," Cordell lied. He was a card sharp, a mechanic.

"Good. We'll get along just fine then."

"How about you double the fine and I leave town?"

"Nope. Then I'd wouldn't have anyone ta play cards with."

Cordell said, "My horse and rig are down at the stable. Send word to hold them until I get out."

"I already did," Marshal Phelps said. "They'll be just fine."

"Thanks, Marshal."

"Say, you wouldn't be lookin' fer work, would ya?"

"I play cards, Marshal. I don't work."

"I was thinkin' about yer gun," the Marshal said. "The Deputy I got now couldn't hit the side of a barn ifn he was in one."

"I'll think it over," Cordell said, although he already knew the answer was no.

"You do thet," the Marshal said. He, too, knew the answer was a no.

A week before the end of his sentence, the Marshal came to Cordell with bad news.

"Somebody stole yer horse," he said. "And yer saddle and saddlebags, too."

"Shit!" Cordell exploded.

"You sure you don't want thet deputy job? It'll pay ya twenty a month."

"Hell, I can make more than that in one night at the Lusty Lady," Cordell said.

"Oh, didn't I tell you, Cordell? Felons can't gamble in Barfield Springs. It's a new town ordinance."

Cordell chuckled. "I see." He thought for a moment. "Well, at least I've got the money I came into town with."

The Marshal looked surprised.

"Money? What money?"

"It's in your desk, with my gun and boot knife."

"Oh thet! That just about covered the funeral for thet Circle D cowboy you drilled. Thet and the money I got fer sellin' yer gun and stuff just about covered it. Not a penny left over."

"I see," Cordell said solemnly.

It wasn't funny anymore. The old Marshal had fixed him good.

On the thirtieth day Jack Cordell stepped from his jail cell a free man. He was dead broke with no horse, gun, or anything else he needed to survive.

"Where ya headed, Cordell?" the Marshal said with a sarcastic smile.

"Hell, I don't have a horse so I guess I ain't headed no place, Marshal."

"We got a vagrancy law in Barfield."

"Oh, of course, Marshal, of course."

"The way I see it, you got two options, Cordell."

"And what are they, Marshal Phelps?"

"Take the deputy job or hop the next cattle train west."

"I might just do that."

"What? Take the deputy job?"

"No. Hop a train west."

With that, Cordell left the jailhouse.

He stood outside in the sun looking around for a moment and finally walked quickly down to the stockyards to the Cattlemen's Association Building. He went inside and saw several cowboys lined up in front of a table where a man sat with a pen and a ledger.

Behind the man, in partial shadow, was another man, a big man with his hat pulled low enough to hide his eyes from view. Cordell could barely make out the thin-lipped wide mouth, large hooked nose, and protruding square chin.

Cordell got in line. He could hear the questions being asked by the man at the table and knew he would have trouble answering them. It was finally his turn.

"Are you in good health?"

"Sure."

"Where have you worked last?"

"I just got out of jail."

"Sorry, we can't use you, mister."

The big man stepped out of the shadows and looked at Cordell and chuckled.

"So you're the little squirt who plugged Turk?"

"He braced me cold. I had no choice," Cordell said.

"You know who I am, friend?"

"Del Oldring? Ramrod of the Circle D?"

"Thet's right, you little shit, and I ought ta squash you like a bug for what you did, you son of a bitch. You cost me one of my best men."

It was strange. Oldring's voice was deep and rusty, yet he was talking to Cordell not in anger but with a sort of mutual admiration.

He looked down at the man at the table. "Hire him."

"Why? He's a gambler. He's no cowpoke."

"Hire him," Oldring repeated. "I got use fer him."

The man at the desk stared at Cordell. "Do you have a horse and outfit?"

"I did when I went to jail, but the Marshal says it was stolen."

Oldring chuckled. "Hell, the old crook sold yer stuff off and kept the money. Nobody stole it." He paused a moment. "I guess you kin have Turk's horse and rig, since you out drew him. It's out at the Circle D. His gun and belt, an' all. Ifn he had a whore you could have her too."

Everyone laughed.

"Sign here," the man at the table said. "Forty a month, food, and bunk. Be back at four. We leave then."

Cordell signed and walked out into the afternoon sun. It was three in the afternoon. He decided to go back to the Marshal's office and tease him a little. Five minutes later he was sitting down next to the Marshal's desk.

"Come back fer that deputy job, Cordell?"

"How much did you say it paid?"

"I think I said twenty a month."

"Twenty a month? Gosh, Marshal, I can make twice that working for the Circle D."

"The Circle D? Del Oldring? You don't wanna sign on with that bunch of sidewinders. They're a bunch of troublemakers. They think they run the town. No, better not sign on with the Circle D."

"I already have, Marshal. I already have," Cordell said casually. "So it looks like I don't have to hop that cattle train west and you can't arrest me for being a vagrant, can you."

The Marshal's face flushed with anger.

"You smart-assed son of a bitch! Get out of my office!" He jumped up, glaring menacingly at Cordell. Cordell just shrugged and got up and walked slowly outside, whistling.

"Be seeing you, Marshal."

Cordell found a double eagle in a corner of one pocket. The Marshal had missed that one. He chuckled and walked up to the beanery and had a bowl of chili and a cup of coffee. An hour later he was sitting in the back of a covered flatbed wagon on its way out to the Circle D Ranch.

Things were starting to look up. The only problem was he was not a cowboy.

4.

There were three other men in the back of the buckboard with Cordell. They were dressed like cowboys and each had a saddlebag One even had a gun and belt. Cordell wore a suit and had nothing.

The Circle D bunkhouse was a long, low wooden building. It was capable of housing forty cowboys when full. At the far end was a door that led to Oldring's room. No one went in there unless they were a member of Oldring's circle of power. These were his own handpicked men, Ned Fargo, Jude Danner, and Milt Renfrew. All were tough cowboys fast on the draw.

Early the next morning, after breakfast, Oldring took Cordell aside.

"Come with me, Cordell," Oldring said. They walked over to a huge barn. Inside was a section where saddles, bridles, and other riding gear were stored. An old man had a shop set up where he repaired saddles and such. When they came in he stopped work stitching a torn saddle.

"Tom, give Cordell here all of Turk's riding gear. All but a lariat. He won't need that."

"I ain't a cowboy," Cordell said.

"I know what you are," Oldring said. "Yer a gambler. I still got a use fer you, so shut up about it. Go git the gear, Tom."

Old Tom nodded and went to where dozens of saddles and other riding gear were neatly lined up on rails or hanging from hooks on the wall. He grabbed a Denver-style saddle with a double cinch and brought it over and dropped it at Cordell's feet.

"Any special harness, mister?"

"Hackamore, if you have one."

Tom nodded and got a leather hackamore with hand carved side conchas. He handed it to Cordell.

Oldring looked at Cordell. "You can stash it under yer bunk. Come on. I'll show you Turk's mount so you and it kin kiss an' make up."

"Sure," Cordell said.

Cordell picked up his gear and followed Oldring out of the barn and next door to the corral. It was a large area fenced off with about eighty horses in it. The mix was pretty good with paints, appaloosas, mustangs, and quarter horses.

"Thet dark brown quarter horse was Turk's," Oldring said, pointing. It took Cordell awhile to pick it out.

"Looks good," Cordell said.

"You two git ta know each other," Oldring said. He left Cordell and started back to the bunkhouse.

"What about his gun?" Cordell shouted.

Oldring chuckled, ignored his question, and kept walking.

Cordell hung the saddle and bridle on the corral fence and climbed up next to it. He sat there watching Turk's horse. It raised its head high and sniffed the air, catching the scent of the saddle. It made its way over to the fence.

"Hi, fellah," Cordell said softly. "We gonna be pals? You wanna go for a ride?"

Cordell slid slowly down inside the corral area beside the horse and gently stroked its forehead and neck. It pressed its head against him. Cordell reached up and got the hackamore from the fence and draped it over the horse's ears and muzzle. After that he got the saddle on and led it out through the corral gate.

For the next few minutes he talked to the animal in a calm voice, stroking it gently. Soon it whinnied and nudged him with its head. That was the result Cordell was waiting for. He tightened the cinches, took the reins in hand, and grabbed onto the saddle horn. With his left foot in the stirrup he eased himself up into the saddle.

After sitting a moment, he tried a knee signal. He pressed his right knee against the horse's shoulder and the animal turned to the left. Cordell tapped him gently with both knees at once and started him walking toward a nearby field. When they reached it the horse stopped and waited for a signal from Cordell.

"Okay, boy, show me what you've got," Cordell said.

He tapped the horse's barrel hard with the sides of his boot heels and it shot like an arrow straight across the field. Cordell's body snapped back against the cantle and for a moment he almost flipped over the animal's flanks. He quickly brought himself upright. He put his head to the wind and let the beast find its level of speed. It made the far end of the field before it finally stopped to feed on the fresh grass.

Cordell got down and rolled a cigarette while the horse ate. When he was finished, he mounted up and they did a slow canter twice around the field. After that, Cordell put the horse back in the corral.

He carried his riding gear into the bunkhouse, found Turk's bunk and stowed the saddle and bridle under it. Finally he went and knocked on Oldring's door.

"Come on in!"

The room had one window which was covered with a blanket. Thick smoke swirled above a table where Oldring and three cowboys, Fargo, Danner, and Renfrew, sat playing cards and smoking under the pale glow of an oil lamp. The room was warm and smelled of sweat.

"Men," Oldring said, "this is the shit-head who drilled Turk."

Fargo gave Cordell a hard look. "Turk musta had a bad day."

Danner, without looking away from his cards, said, "We should hang the son of a bitch, boss."

"Maybe later," Oldring chuckled. "Right now I got a use fer him."

Oldring put his cards down and stood up. He stretched his six-foot-three frame then came over and looked down at Cordell. He stared hard at him. His breath smelled of whiskey and he was a little unsteady on his feet.

"Yer gonna earn yer keep here, Cordell. I'll have a special use fer you later. In the meantime you don't leave the ranch unless I say so."

"Is that all?" Cordell asked casually.

"No, that ain't all, smart ass!" Oldring spat out the words. "You don't go near the ranch house. You don't even look at it. And you never talk to Mr. Denton or Mrs. Denton. Is thet clear? Is thet damn clear?"

"Yeah. Sure."

"You cross me, Cordell, and I'll put a bullet right between your eyes!" Oldring poked Cordell in the forehead with a finger. "Now get the hell outta here an' stay where I kin see ya."

"Sure thing, boss," Cordell said with a smile.

Oldring sat down. Cordell went out and laid on his bunk.

The cowboy on the bunk to his right dropped his penny dreadful and looked over at Cordell.

"Welcome to the Circle D, friend. My name is Caleb." He said with a southern accent.

"I'm Jack." They shook hands.

"Supper is at seven," Caleb said. "Breakfast is at five. Monday is laundry day. Payday is at the end of the month. You ain't no cowboy, are you?"

"No."

"So, what exactly are you, pal?"

"Right now I'm not sure," Cordell said with a chuckle.

A few minutes after Cordell laid down for a nap, Ned Fargo came out of Oldring's room and kicked his bunk.

"Get up, Cordell," Fargo said. "I got a job fer you."

Cordell followed Fargo outside. They walked over to a large open shed where the range stove was set up. There were three long plank-board picnic tables there. The range cook and his helper were preparing supper.

"Hey, Cookie," Fargo said. "Oldring wants ya ta work this new guy's ass off."

Cookie was a skinny, whiskered, back-bent old man, once a cowboy but now a cook. He had a red bandana draped around his neck and was sweating heavily over the range stove. The other one was a cowboy on kitchen duty peeling turnips over a large pot.

The cook looked at Fargo and nodded.

Before leaving, Fargo took Cordell aside. "You kilt Elroy Turk an' he was my friend. Once Oldring is finished with yer rotten ass I'm gonna brace you and kill you. I want you to think about thet."

Cordell shrugged and said nothing. Fargo left.

The cook had Cordell pump up several pails of water from the cistern then set him down to chop up carrots and onions. Before long his eyes were burning and tears were running down his face.

"What the hell you cryin' about, fellah?" the cook asked. They all laughed at Cordell.

At seven the supper bell sounded and the cowboys came out of the bunkhouse to eat turnip venison stew, peach cobbler, and coffee. Cordell, the cook, and the helper were the last ones to eat. It was almost ten in the evening when the cook released Cordell after telling him to come back at four in the morning.

When Cordell walked into the bunkhouse he was met with chuckles and crude remarks. Words like carpetbagger, underwear salesman, and paper pusher floated around the room. They correctly guessed he wasn't a cowboy and knew he was there only because Oldring wanted him there.

After a while they settled down and ignored him. A small group started a card game. He rolled a cigarette and went over to watch. They made idle talk among themselves. Cordell listened and soon the subject of cards came up.

"There's this guy at the Lusty Lady who is the best at cards I ever saw," one cowboy said. "He sure is good."

"Yeah, I know who you mean," another said. "He's there every night. He's really lucky."

"Maybe he's cheatin'," still another said. "Somebody oughtta call him out."

"Somebody already did, but they didn't find nothin' up his sleeve," someone else said.

"He's a mechanic," Cordell said casually. "You can't catch him."

"A what?" the first cowboy asked, giving Cordell a 'who the hell asked you' look.

"A mechanic. A card virtuoso," Cordell said.

"What the hell are you talkin' about, ass hole?" one said.

"Here, I'll show you. Move over."

Cordell got a chair and eased in between two cowboys. He took a fresh deck of cards from the card box on the table. The cowboys put their cards face down to watch him.

"This is called false shuffling," Cordell said as he shuffled the cards. His hands move quickly in the pale light of the oil lamp above the table. "I'm not really mixing the cards. It just looks that way."

"What good is thet?" someone asked.

"It's good because I've got my aces where I can get at them." He peeled off the four aces, face up. "See?"

Now he had their full attention.

"How this guy deals depends on how many people are playing. Four, five, six, whatever. Right now I'm dealing from the bottom of the deck but you can't notice it."

They watched closely.

"He can put all the aces on top and keep them there while he bottom deals, or he can put them on the bottom as he top deals. He can do anything he wants."

Cordell dealt himself eight cards and turned them face up. They were four aces and four deuces.

Someone whistled in wonderment.

"Or, if he has a partner, he can deal him a winning hand any time he feels like it, to take the pressure off himself."

Cordell gathered the cards, shuffled them, and dealt the cowboy next to him a poker hand of three aces and two deuces.

"The son of a bitch," someone whispered.

"Ain't there no way ta catch the bastard?" another asked.

Cordell shrugged. "Maybe. Does he cut the cards himself or does he let the man to the left cut them?"

"He mostly lets the guy on the right cut them," someone said.

"That might be his partner," Cordell said. "Usually the player on the left gets to cut." Cordell paused a moment for effect. "Look, when he sets the deck down, before anyone can cut it, one of you have to grab it and turn it over so the cards are face up. Look to see if the aces are together on the top or bottom." He added. "When you do this, be careful. He might just pull a derringer and plug you."

The room went quiet. Every cowboy in the bunkhouse watched Cordell's seminar on catching card cheats.

"Thanks, friend," several cowboys said.

"Much obliged," the first cowboy said. Several reached over to pat Cordell on the back or shake his hand.

"Who the hell are you, mister?" someone asked.

"I know who he is," another said. "He's Jack Cordell. He plugged Red Hardy in a card game in Cheneyville some years ago."

"Is thet true, mister?"

"That was a long time ago. I caught him palming aces. He was a lousy poker player."

A chuckle rippled throughout the room.

Cordell put the deck back in the card box and went back to his bunk feeling a little better now. He decided to wait until Oldring called on him for that special job.

5.

George Denton, owner of the Circle D Ranch, was originally from Boston. He inherited a small ship building company from his parents there but his heart was not in ships or the sea. It was in cowboys. He was an avid reader of western pulp magazines and novels. He dreamt of the west, the open spaces, and man against nature, even though he never rode a horse or shot a gun.

One day an investment banker friend told George about the booming cattle trade out west. Bankers, investors, and businessmen from the east and beyond were going there in large numbers. Men of high social status, called gentlemen ranchers, saw it as a chance to increase their fortunes and get away from city life. Tenderfoot ranching was in vogue and to George Denton it sounded very exciting. It was exactly what he was dreaming of all these years.

The nicest part was a rancher could sit back and watch it all happen. It was a very simple, primitive system. Cows ate the grass and multiplied and once a year they were sold at market.

As for the ignorant uneducated cowboys, they worked for practically nothing. All you had to do was hire a ramrod, a foreman to keep everything going smoothly. Names like ramrod, and other western terms, fascinated George Denton.

After many inquiries and some research, Denton, at the age of thirty and unmarried, left Boston for an exploratory trip to a place he had heard of called Barfield Springs, in faraway mid-west Texas. He had written to a realtor in Barfield and arranged to go there to look over some properties that were up for foreclosure.

When he arrived at Barfield Springs, Denton took Mr. Reed, the realtor, to dinner at the Emerald Hotel. After a fine meal and several drinks, they went over to see Mr. Patterson at the Cattlemen's Union Bank.

Under Mr. Reed's guidance, Mr. Patterson suggested three possible purchases. They were all small ranches whose owners were months behind in their loan payments and were being foreclosed on. Any one of these ranches would be a good financial investment for a business minded person.

George Denton jumped at the opportunity of making his lifelong dream come true, a ranch bearing his name. So he quickly sealed the deal on the largest of the three ranches.

But one problem quickly arose.

He had a ranch but no one to manage it. All the hands left with the previous owner. None of them wanted to work for a carpetbagger, a city slicker, a tenderfoot.

All, except one. Del Oldring.

Big, towering, broad shouldered Del Oldring had been a quiet, lowly, humble cowboy working on the ranch for twenty dollars a month, taking orders from a ramrod he didn't like. So when the crew of the Circle L left, he stayed in the shadows until the coast was clear and approached the new owner, George Denton.

"I'm yer man, Mr. Denton," Oldring said. "I'll ramrod this outfit fer you and make it the best hereabouts, ifn you'll have me. All I ask is sixty a month."

"But there is no one to ramrod, Mr. Oldring," George pointed out. "Everyone has deserted me, except the Mexican cook, Conchatta."

"Don't you worry none about thet, sir," Oldring said. "I'll hire a new crew at forty a month an' they'll be the best crew around."

"Alright, Mr. Oldring, it's a deal," Denton said.

Oldring was true to his word. In one month he hired on fifteen cowboys, enough to start with. He also took time out to teach George Denton how to ride a western horse and shoot both a Winchester and a shotgun. The two soon went hunting and riding. They became close friends.

Oldring also became very protective of his employer and saw to it that no one bothered him with petty problems. And that was fine with Denton. Life had never been better.

After six months, Denton returned to Boston to finalize the sale of his ship building business and say goodbye to his friends.

They all commented on how robust and healthy he looked. Being a rancher agreed with him. Denton felt proud of what he and Oldring had accomplished together. He exaggerated glowingly about life in the savage wilds, about the isolation and hardships. They listened and loved it.

When his business was completed, Denton said his farewells and headed west again. At a stopover in Chicago he met a woman by accident as he bumped into her on the street. Perhaps she had bumped into him. He wasn't sure. She was stunningly beautiful and charming and he took her to dinner. Her name was Val, short for Valerie.

Denton wined and dined and courted Val for two weeks. When he returned to Barfield Springs and the Circle D Ranch he brought her as his wife.

George Denton's life was now perfect. All his dreams had come true. A plain looking man, small and thin, but intelligent, now had the most beautiful wife and the best run ranch in the area, thanks to his ramrod big Del Oldring.

Denton enjoyed hunting. He had a gun rack in his study with several rifles and shotguns.

He took the time to teach Val what Oldring had taught him about hunting small game. Soon they were going out together into the fields with a couple of cowboys to flush the game. Some days they brought down twenty or thirty birds. It was great sport and Conchatta, the cook, would serve roast quail and pheasant to all the cowboys.

Denton was well respected by his neighboring ranchers and he treated them well. He shared his grass and water with them. As far as the late spring cattle drive was concerned, he left that to Oldring and his cowboys.

Life was very good for George Denton until the day he had the accident.

It happened out in the field beyond the ranch house. He, Val, and two of the cowboys came over a rise on horseback and surprised a covey of quail. Instead of dismounting first, Denton shot from the saddle. The loud boom of the double barrel shotgun spooked the horse. It bucked, sending him flying and spinning to the ground. He landed hard on his back. He tried to get up but couldn't.

One cowboy rushed back to get a buckboard. When he returned they loaded George in the back and took him home. Val sent a man to town for Doctor Barnes. After a most thorough examination, the doctor advised sending for a spine expert. One finally came from San Antonio. His diagnosis was dire. George Denton would never walk or ride again.

After the accident Denton became depressed. He wanted to sell the Circle D Ranch and go back to Boston. At least there he could get the best medical attention and maybe one day he could run a business, even if in a wheel chair.

But Val didn't want that. They argued over it a lot until she finally gave George her ultimatum: If he sold the ranch she would leave him. He loved her too dearly ever to do anything to hurt her, so he gave in to her demand. Whatever she wanted, she got. George Denton was a beaten man.

After the accident, Val Denton gradually took control of George and the ranch. It could just as well have been called the Circle V. She isolated George and kept everyone away from him under the guise of protecting his health.

But there was one problem, and that was Del Oldring.

From the start she let the ramrod know she detested him and wanted him gone. She asked George to fire him, but he wouldn't.

One day the two clashed openly.

"Mr. Oldring," Val said, "the Circle D no longer wants or requires your services. Here's five-hundred dollars. I would appreciate your leaving today."

Oldring chuckled. "No ma'am, I ain't leavin'. I built this ranch and I'm gonna make sure you don't ruin it."

"Must I call the Marshal, sir, and have you physically removed?"

"You don't want ta do thet, ma'am."

"Is that a threat, sir?"

"If I go, all the cowboys will go with me," Oldring said. "You ain't got the smarts ta run a ranch, bein' a city gal."

She glared at him. He had stopped her in her tracks and she wanted him dead.

"Perhaps," Val said. "We shall see." She turned to walk away but stopped with her back to Oldring. "One thing, though. You are no longer welcome in my house, so please keep your ugly face down at the bunkhouse, sir!"

She walked quickly up to the ranch house. She didn't see the way Oldring glared at her.

6.

Five miles west of Barfield Springs, Kid Breen saw that the cowboy named Sid was tailing him. He stopped and whistled back, then waited until he caught up.

"You following me?"

"Sort of."

Breen chuckled. "A lot of good thet'll do ya. I'm plumb lost."

"Well, I ain't."

The kid looked at Sid for a moment. "You got fired fer stickin' up fer me, didn't ya?"

"I reckon."

"Well, I'm sorry about thet."

"Hell, I didn't like those ass holes anyway," Sid said.

"So, whatta ya think we should do, partner?"

Sid liked being called partner. "There's an old line shack up a ways. We kin make coffee there an' figure it out."

They rode on for another five miles and found the place close to a stream. The kid made a fire while Sid went to fill the coffee pot. By the time it was dark they were sitting across from each other drinking coffee.

"I'm on a mission," the kid said, sounding mysterious.

"What kind a mission?" Sid asked. He sounded a bit awe struck.

"I'm lookin' fer a man."

"You gonna kill 'em?"

"No, I jest wanna tell him somethin', is all."

"Oh." Sid sounded disappointed. "Whatcha gonna tell him?"

"I can't tell nobody else, jest him."

They were quiet for a while, listening to the night sounds.

"Kin you wrangle?" Sid asked.

"I reckon."

"There's a small spread about fifteen miles west. The Bar C. I'm gonna see ifn they'll take me on."

"I might jest go with ya, if it's okay."

"Sure."

"My name is Sid. Sid Turner."

"Mine is Tobey. Tobey Breen."

"Yeah, I heard," Sid chuckled.

They spent the night in the ruins of the old line shack huddled alongside the fire making small talk until they fell asleep. At sunrise they had jerky, hardtack, and coffee.

"I can't stand much more of thet salted jerky," the kid said as they rode off for the Bar C Ranch.

"The food at the Circle D was great," Sid said. "Ol' Conchatta, the Mexican cook, could sure dish it up."

They rode over land lush with grass and scrub oaks. The sun was warm and clouds were building on the horizon. Birds flew in flocks above them. Crows cawed in the pines. A deer ran across their path, yards in front of them.

The ground beneath them started to slope downward and after a while the two riders saw the Bar C in the distance. They stopped to watch the cowhands come out of the small bunkhouse and go over to the barn to get their saddles and gear. They took it to the corral next to the barn, and saddled up and rode out.

A lone man stayed behind, watching them leave.

"Whose thet?" the kid asked.

"That's ol' Bern, the ramrod," Sid said. "Bern Langley. He's a cantankerous old fart. Kin hardly walk any more. Never gits off his horse except to eat, sleep, an' piss."

The kid chuckled.

By the time they got down to the yard they found old Bern hitching a horse up to a buckboard. They dismounted and Bern stared at the kid.

"Need any help?" the kid offered.

"So yer what all the talk in town is about?"

"You heard?" Sid asked before the kid could answer.

Bern turned to Sid. "Yeah. A couple of our boys was in town at the Lusty Lady. They saw the whole thing go down."

"We're lookin' for a place to roost," Sid said.

"The kid, maybe. You? Nope! You kin take yer ass back to the Circle D where you belong."

"I can't," Sid said. "They're lookin' ta brace me if they catch me alone."

"We're pards," the kid said.

"Yeah," Sid boasted, "we're pards! We're like two peas in a pod, Bern! Haw!"

The old man mulled it over for a moment then chuckled. "Hell, why not. I could use a fool like you, Sid, ta clean the shithouse out once a week."

Suddenly a man and a woman came out onto the front porch of the ranch house and stared down at them.

The kid quickly noticed the contrast between the two. She was plain-faced, had short, rippling red hair, and was dressed in a man's shirt, vest, trousers, and boots. The man had coal-black hair and was exceedingly handsome with a pencil mustache, but was somewhat delicate looking. He wore a suit and looked more like a salesman than a rancher.

The woman stayed in place while the man came down the steps and over to them. Bern introduced the man as Larry Conroy, owner of the Bar C.

"Mr. Conroy," old Bern said. "Seein' as we lost three men last week, I figured maybe we could use some replacements? At least two more, sir?" He waited for a reply but got none, so he went on. "The kid here is the one thet ventilated all those Circle D cowpokes. I figure we might be able ta use him."

The rancher stared blankly at the kid.

"Could I talk to you a minute Bern?" Conroy said with raised eyebrows.

"Why sure ya kin, Mr. Conroy."

Larry Conroy took the old ramrod aside out of earshot and spoke to him in a low voice.

The woman on the porch stared intensely across the yard at the kid. She didn't look too happy.

"So you're the one who killed those three innocent men yesterday, are you?" she said loudly.

"Yes, ma'am. I sure did."

"You seem pretty casual about it, young man. Is it something you're proud of?"

"Proud? No, man. I was jest trying ta stop them from killin' me first. I'm real sorry I had ta do it."

Suddenly a young girl came out onto the porch. Her hair was red like her mothers, but straight and tied up in a bow. It fell to her shoulders. She wore a pink cotton dress and was beautiful. The kid smiled and tipped his hat. She smiled back.

The kid chuckled happily.

Mrs. Conroy turned to the girl and said, with authority, "Go inside, Jilly-girl!"

The girl retreated into the house.

"You sure have a purdy daughter, ma'am," the kid said.

"She's not for your eyes to see, young man," Nora Conroy said sharply. "And that's the closest you'll ever get to her."

Larry Conroy got on the buckboard seat, clicked his tongue, and moved it up to the porch steps. The girl came out carrying some books. She got in beside him and they drove off. Nora Conroy went into the house.

"Where are they headed?" the kid asked.

"She helps with the teachin' over at the rancher's school house," Bern said.

"Maybe I should go get some learnin' over there," the kid said.

"Me, too," Sid chuckled. "I'm plumb ignorant!"

Old Bern looked at them both and shook his head. Sid understood immediately.

"Oh, oh," Sid said. "We jest got turned down."

"Sorry," the old ramrod said. "The boss thinks it's best not ta hire you two. Seein' as what you did to the Circle D. He says he don't want no trouble."

"I guess I'm poison everywhere now," the kid sighed. "But, why not take Sid?"

"Same reason. He don't want no trouble from Oldring," Bern said. "Best ifn you two jest ride on out. Nobody is gonna hire either one of you."

Sid sighed and was about to mount up when he stopped and said, "Say, old timer, mind ifn we stay at the north-end line shack fer a couple a days? Until we figure out what we're gonna do an' where we're gonna go? Could ya give us thet, maybe?"

Bern turned the request over in his mind. He finally nodded. "Okay, but lay low out there. Don't get caught. It'll be my ass, ifn ya do."

"Sure, don't worry," Sid said. "We'll be as invisible as a ghost and jest as quiet."

The kid chuckled. "Send that cute little pixie up there with a couple of apple pies, if ya kin."

"Yeah," Sid said, "an' a basket of fried chicken, too!"

The two young cowboys chuckled and smiled. Old Bern wagged a finger at them.

"Don't even think about Miss Jilly, boys," he said with a scowl. "Mrs. Conroy keeps a double barrel shot gun handy fer critters sech as you two!"

"Oops!" the kid said. "Sorry about that, friend!"

"Vamoose! Both of you! Git!" Bern growled.

The kid and Sid Turner mounted and headed out for the north-end line shack.

7.

Larry Conroy once worked as a shoe salesman in Chicago. He was handsome and popular with the ladies so he continued to play the field even after he got married and had three children. One day the pressure of family life got too much for him so he hopped a train of empty cattle cars that were headed west to be refilled.

The cars were full of riff raff and dregs of humanity on the way west to get rich panning for gold. Some were on the run from the law and others, like Conroy, were running from life in general.

He kept a low profile and somehow managed to reach Barfield Springs alive and with his good looks intact. He got a job at Stoddard's Mercantile where he stocked shelves and clerked.

It was there that he eventually met the widow Nora Barnes and her daughter Jilly. Nora owned the small but successful Bar B Ranch west of town. Conroy immediately saw her as a way to climb the social ladder in Barfield Springs.

Nora Barnes was not what anyone would call a pretty woman but she did have the look of a sturdy pioneer woman from good strong stock. She smelled like fresh air and let her curly, red, unruly hair have its own way. She had a finely chiseled nose, blue eyes, and a seductive smile. Her cheeks were flecked with large brown freckles, giving her a youthful tomboy look even at the age of thirty-five. She also could do a man's work and fire a gun.

Her late husband was killed in a stampeded on a trail drive when Jilly was only five years old.

Conroy didn't know or even care about what kind of woman Nora was. What he did know was that in the widow Barnes he saw a chance to become more than just a store clerk earning five dollars a week. And that's all she meant to him. Nothing more. He wasn't in love with her.

Nora however was overwhelmed by Conroy's attention and charm. She let him slide into her life little by little. She did the courting by taking the buckboard to town, picking him up, and bringing him to the ranch for a picnic or dinner. She taught him how to ride and hook up a buckboard.

Old Bern and the other cowboys at the Bar B saw what was happening. They didn't like it but said nothing, although they did make remarks behind Conroy's back. They let him know he would never be one of them. He was city and he smelled city.

When Nora and Conroy finally got married, the cowhands knew they were in for a hard time. One day he walked into the bunkhouse and fired two cowboy at random, just to put the fear of God into them all. After that everyone gave Conroy a wide birth and stayed out of his way.

Conroy especially enjoyed his new status as rancher and attended the monthly meetings at the Cattlemen's Association Building in Barfield Springs.

It was there he learned to smoke expensive cigars and drink mixed drinks such as bourbon and tonic. Although he was unable to engage in any serious discussions about cattle diseases or infestations, he did have the satisfaction of knowing he was the handsomest man in the room, as seen in the huge mirror behind the bar.

As soon as she heard about George Denton's hunting accident Nora suggested they visit him at the Circle D Ranch. It was the neighborly thing to do.

They rode into the yard of the Circle D and dismounted just as Del Oldring, the ranch ramrod, was coming out of the barn. He stopped and tipped his hat to Nora. When Conroy held out his hand to introduce himself, Oldring ignored it and walked away towards the bunkhouse.

"Rude bastard," Conroy muttered.

"He's old west," Nora said.

Conroy shrugged. He didn't know that Oldring had pegged him for a dandy. Oldring hated dandies.

As they went up the porch steps. Valerie Denton met them at the top. When she and Larry Conroy saw each other it was love at first sight.

Everyone else around them suddenly seemed dull and common. Right then and there their eyes spoke the silent words that their hearts felt. They knew they were perfect for each other. They were superior human beings surrounded by inferior people. They couldn't take their eyes off one another. Nothing and no one else mattered.

And Nora Conroy saw it all happening right there in front of her and she couldn't do a thing to stop it. She never experienced such a helpless feeling before.

Inside, Nora sat talking to George while Larry and Valerie drifted off somewhere for almost an hour. When they returned Mrs. Denton was flush-faced. So was Larry. It was obvious something happened between them.

"I was showing Larry the new stallion you bought me, George," Valerie said. "He was quite impressed."

"Yes," Larry said, trying to sound knowledgeable. "It's quite a beast." He avoided Nora's eyes.

George Denton, too, knew something had happened between his wife and Larry Conroy. It was obvious by the guilty looks on their faces.

Later, as they rode back to the Bar C, Nora could smell the scent of Valerie Denton on her husband. It was like a stab to the heart, the ultimate betrayal of trust and love.

As they went along, Larry Conroy babbled on and on about what a wonderful talented woman Valerie Denton was.

Suddenly he said, "She's very pretty, isn't she?"

"If you like painted ladies," Nora shot back sharply.

After that they went on in complete silence with Larry Denton wondering what he had said wrong.

8.

The very next day after Nora and he had visited the Circle D, Larry Conroy became a busy man. Pretending to go out to check on the line shacks, he met with George Denton's wife at a designated landmark, a huge dead tree by a pile of rocks near the dividing line between the two ranches. After that he invented more excuses to ride out alone, such as checking on the water holes or the cattle or the cowhands.

Once to avoid suspicion and to throw Nora off her guard, he stayed around the ranch house a whole week before going off at night to the rancher's meeting at the Cattlemen's Association Building in town. He showed up, stayed for a short time and left to secretly meet Valerie at the Emerald Hotel.

A week later while going to meet her at the big tree, he decided to take a shortcut that led past the north-end line shack. He saw two horses hobbled in a grassy patch nearby. He hid in a pine stand and watched. When he discovered it was the kid and Sid Turner, he wondered how long they had been there.

At first Conroy was angry and was about to turn them out but decided he couldn't waste the time. He wondered if old Bern knew of it and concluded he probably did. At any rate he didn't want any distractions at the moment. He would settle this at a more appropriate time.

Valerie Denton became an addiction for Larry Conroy. She dominated him and he was almost in awe of her. One day her dark side revealed itself.

"Oh, Larry, darling," she said. "We can't go on like this forever."

"Yes, it's awkward, isn't it, Val?" Larry replied.

"Just think what we could accomplish together if we were both free."

"What do you mean, love?"

"If I was sole owner of the circle D and you were sole owner of the Bar C, think what that would mean."

Larry Conroy thought about that for a moment and said, "Yes, we could marry and have the biggest ranch in the area."

"Exactly! We could let others run it and invest the profits to make more money. We could become rich!"

Larry Conroy saw the wisdom in her words.

"The best part is," she continued, "we wouldn't even have to stay here all the time. We could live in Chicago or New York or even California. Visit here once or twice a year."

It all sounded good. They could become absentee owners of a thriving business.

"Yes!" Larry suddenly saw the logic of it all. He would be wealthy and never have to work. Let the dumb cowboys like Oldring and old Bern do that.

Suddenly he laughed. "I don't see how that's going to happen, Val. We're both married."

"Yes," Valerie Denton said softly, "but accidents do happen, don't they?"

Larry Conroy felt a chill run up his backbone.

9.

Del Oldring was a man of integrity and loyalty. His boss, George Denton, depended on him to ramrod the Circle D and he had done so in a professional way. Oldring saw to it that Denton was never bothered by petty problems, or even some serious ones. They were about as close as owner and hired hand could be.

Oldring taught the tenderfoot the way of the cowboy, to shoot and ride just like them, so he could be a decent rancher and appreciate the hard work that cowboys did each day.

The ramrod also had another code he lived by. A code which he installed in his men. If one of the Circle D cowboys were shot down, no matter who, where, or why, the act would not go unanswered and unpunished. They would find the guilty party and deal him swift justice. Usually by hanging.

The Marshal complained but he was outnumbered by too many Circle D boys to prevent it.

One more thing Del Oldring could not tolerate was someone standing between him and his benefactor George Denton. No cowhand would ever approach Denton or speak to him without going to Oldring first. Every cowhand on the Circle D knew these rules and abided by them. Their loyalty was to Oldring first, then Denton. Oldring was the brand and they rode for him without question.

But two things had occurred to upset the status quo. And both these problems had to be taken care of.

First was the killing of the Circle D cowboys Lem, Zeke, and Curt by the kid from Del Rio. Oldring vowed to find and hang the kid, and had men out listening and looking for any clue to his whereabouts. It was only a matter of time, and Oldring could be patient when he had to be.

Second was the problem of Valerie Denton. She put up a wall between him and George, blocking his every attempt to talk to him. She also treated the ramrod with utter contempt. To her he was just another hired hand. She, too, was patient and waited for a valid reason to fire Oldring.

Knowing this, Oldring treaded carefully keeping his distance from her. He also put his spies on her. One in the house and one on the outside that followed her constantly.

It was the outside spy that eventually paid off.

"She's meeting up with Larry Conroy," the spy said. "In the woods mostly, but sometimes at the hotel in town. Once I got close enough to hear them talking."

"Oh?"

"Yeah. She wanted to meet in the north-end line shack but he said no, they couldn't go near the place because somebody was in it. You know what I think?"

"That the kid is hidin' there? Yeah, so do I," Oldring chuckled. He couldn't believe his luck. "Good work, Jesse."

At that point Oldring made two decisions. He'd send his men out to hang the kid while he would take care of Valerie Denton once and for all.

And he might as well take care of Larry Conroy while he was at it.

10.

Del Oldring grabbed the hanging rope and called Canfield, Fowler, and the new man, Cordell, aside.

"I want you three ta go check out the north-end Bar C line shack."

"What's up, boss?" Canfield asked.

"Thet kid might be layin' low up there."

"Does the Bar C know about it?" Fowler asked.

"I think they might."

"What if we find the kid?" Canfield asked.

"Hang him and bring his horse and gear back here."

Oldring turned to Cordell and tossed him the rope he used to measure out justice. "Cordell, yer new here. Here's yer chance ta prove yer one of us. You get to hang the kid. Ifn you ain't got the grit fer it you kin wrangle someplace else."

Cordell caught the rope and shrugged.

"Is he the one who plugged your three men a while back?" Cordell asked.

"Yep," Canfield interjected. "Thet's him."

"Then I guess he's got it coming," Cordell said.

"Alright, then," Oldring said. "Go git it done an' make sure nobody knows about it."

"How about Turk's gun," Cordell said. "You promised me all of Turk's gear. I might need it in case the kid has help."

"Alright, but I want it back after the job," Oldring said.

He went to his room in the bunkhouse and came back with a belt and gun. Cordell checked it out and nodded. He buckled it on. Now he had it all, gun and horse.

They saddled up and rode out.

They headed north-west going past the field where Denton had his accident and on into a stand of tall pines. On the far side of that was cattle country, mostly wide open except for a few low hills. A fast flowing stream glistened in the sunlight off to their right. Beyond that they entered a large grassy bowl full of cattle with hills rising on the sides.

They saw some cowboys near a line shack in the distance and waved but kept going.

Near evening they stopped.

"This is where the Circle D ends," Canfield explained to Cordell. "The Bar C line shack is about two miles over that ridge line."

"Let's wait until dark and jump 'em," Fowler said.

"That's jest what I was a thinkin'," Canfield replied. "We kin catch 'em by surprise when they're asleep. Whatta you think, Cordell?"

Cordell shrugged. "It's your call, Canfield."

They dismounted, hobbled their mounts near some aspen saplings where there was also some grass. Fowler pulled a bottle of whiskey from his saddlebag. They walked over and sat down with their backs to some trees. Fowler and Canfield started drinking.

Cordell pulled his hat down low and pretended to be asleep.

"Looks like the jailbird is takin' a beauty nap," Fowler chuckled.

"Keep yer eye on him, Fowler," Canfield said. "I don't know him well enough ta trust him yet an' neither do you."

"The rumor in the bunkhouse is thet he's only gonna stay long enough to buy a horse an' rig, and then move on."

Canfield took a drink and handed the bottle back to Fowler. "All the more reason ta keep an eye on him. He ain't never gonna be one of us, pal."

"Thet's fer sure," Fowler said. "Thet's fer dang sure."

Cordell smiled under the shadow of his hat.

Fowler and Canfield stopped talking. A far off coyote started howling at the setting sun and soon others joined in the chorus. Night birds and bats began to fly low across the landscape. Somewhere frogs croaked and crickets chirped.

Canfield and Fowler began nodding. After a while they slid down slowly on the ground and dozed off. Eventually they were in a deep sleep.

Hours passed by.

"What?" Fowler said. Cordell was standing over him.

"Get the hell up!" Cordell kicked Canfield.

"What the hell!" Canfield rubbed his eyes and yawned. "What time is it?"

"Almost sun up," Cordell said.

"Shit!" Canfield jumped up and Fowler did too.

They quickly mounted up and rode the first mile at a fast pace, slowed down to a trot, and then a fast walk. Finally Canfield stopped and dismounted.

"It's jest over that slope," he said, pointing.

They tied their horses to some pines and checked their guns. Cordell got the hanging rope off his saddle horn.

The started off at a slow walk and went down the slope. Cordell saw the line shack fifty yards away, in a small clearing. It had only one door in the front and two small side windows.

All three came around the rear to the front, crouching low with their guns drawn. Canfield and Fowler listened a moment then kicked the door open and rushed in shouting as Cordell stood watch outside. In a few minutes they brought the kid and Sid out in their long johns with no boots on.

Cordell went into the line shack and came out with their boots. He tossed them on the ground.

"They won't need no boots," Canfield growled. "Not where they're a goin'."

"A little professional courtesy," Cordell chuckled. "Anyway, their feet smell bad enough to knock over a buffalo."

The kid and Sid scrambled to get their boots on.

Fowler looked at Sid. "You shoulda left when you had the chance, Sid."

"Is the rope fer me too Fowler?" Sid asked.

Fowler laughed, shaking his head.

"Naw, jest the kid," Canfield cut in. "You git ta draw on me. It's more fun."

Sid sort of chuckled nervously. "Hell, Canfield, you know I'm a slow draw. You kin beat me by a mile."

"Draw on me, mister," the kid said calmly, smiling. "Or are ya too afraid?"

"No, kid, yer gonna taste the rope," Canfield sneered. He turned to Cordell, "Let's see him dance."

Cordell took a few steps towards the kid. "What's your name?"

The kid chuckled. "What's yer's, mister?"

Canfield chuckled. "Sassy little brat, ain't he?"

"My name is Cordell. Jack Cordell, kid."

The kid suddenly looked surprised. "No shit! I been lookin' fer you, mister!"

Cordell grinned, and then frowned. "That's clever, kid, but it ain't gonna help you any."

"You ever been down around Del Rio way?"

"Sure, so what?"

"You know a woman there named Freckle-face Fanny?"

"What about her?"

"She's my mom," the kid said.

For a moment Cordell was off balance. "Nice try kid, but you're still going to hang."

"I ain't lyin'. Honest injin!" the kid insisted. "I got her picture right in there, in my shirt pocket. You wanna see it?"

Cordell's eyes flickered with indecision for a second then settled down to a stare.

"You gonna talk the kid ta death or hang him," Canfield growled. "Quit messin' around with him."

"Hell, I think I'll just shoot the little fart," Cordell said.

Cordell tossed the hanging rope in Canfield's face. Canfield was startled for a second but ducked the rope and quickly fired off a shot as Cordell drew. His bullet took Cordell's hat off. Cordell dropped low, drew, and shot Canfield in the chest.

As Canfield went down, Fowler pulled his gun and got off a shot that creased Cordell in the left rib cage.

Suddenly Sid ran at Fowler yelling, "Hey Fowler! Over here, you son of a bitch!"

Fowler turned quickly. Off balance, he snapped off a quick shot that hit Sid across his right shoulder.

"Over her, Fowler!" Cordell shouted and fired from a kneeling positon. His shot caught Fowler in the upper right chest and spun him sideways. Fowler fired a wild shot into the ground and collapsed alongside Canfield.

For a few seconds there was only the dying echoes of the duel. Cordell stood up and reloaded his Colt. He didn't seem to notice his side was bleeding. Sid was sitting on the ground holding his shoulder.

"Let's go inside," the kid said. He helped Sid up and they all went in the line shack.

Sid sat down on a cot while the kid opened the medicine box. It had a bottle of toothache drops, a bottle of iodine, and a roll of cotton bandage. After he attended to Sid, Cordell wrapped the bandage a couple of times around his own waist.

"Let's see that picture, kid," Cordell said.

The kid picked up his shirt and reached into a pocket. He handed a small, wrinkled, faded photo to Cordell who held it up to the light and examined it.

"Yeah. Long ago. She was married to a friend of mine."

He handed the picture back to the kid. "I lost track of them. His name was Breen."

"Yeah, Jim Breen. He was my dad. He died a year before she did, robbing a bank."

"Sorry to hear that, kid."

"He was a no account bastard," the kid said. "She was too good for him." The kid put the picture away. "She talked about you. How you were fast on the draw. That you were a legend."

"How did you find me?"

The kid chuckled. "Hell, I didn't! You found me, with a hangin' rope in yer hand! Figure that one out."

Cordell shook his head. "I can't. Nobody can." He mused for a moment. "I almost married her, but he beat me out."

"Yeah. She told me," the kid recalled. "I wish you had."

Cordell looked at Sid. He was quiet and pale.

"Your friend doesn't look so good, kid."

The kid glanced over at Sid, and then stood up. "We gotta git him some help. Come on."

"Take me ta see ol' Bern," Sid said. He had trouble standing. "He'll help me."

The kid quickly dressed then helped Sid with his clothes.

"What'll we do with the bodies?" the kid asked Cordell.

"Tie them on their horses and send them running. They know the way back."

They got the horses and tied Fowler and Canfield across the saddles then sent them off with a slap on the flanks. They watched until they were out of sight and went into the line shack for Sid.

They got him on his horse and used what was left of the hanging rope to tie his feet in the stirrups and his hands to the saddle horn. The kid took his reins and they started off for the Bar C Ranch.

"You okay, pard?" the kid asked, looking back.

"Hell, never been better, pard," Sid muttered as he slumped forward over the saddle horn.

Cordell came alongside. "Don't stop. I'll keep an eye on him."

They headed for the Bar C.

11.

It was late at night. Del Oldring sat alone in the Lusty Lady Saloon thinking. He was not so much thinking as he was trying to sort things out.

Foremost on his mind was the Circle D Ranch.

Since he became ramrod of the Circle D, Oldring was George Denton's adviser in all matters concerning the ranch. While Denton took care of the financial and social aspects of the ranch, Oldring made sure everything went smoothly on a day-to-day basis.

As far as the cowboys went, Oldring had more or less paternal relationship with them.

Curt, Lem, and Zeke signed on with Oldring way back when Denton became the new owner, and they had been with him ever since. When there was a hard job to be done, they were the ones Oldring picked to do it, especially on cattle drives and roundups.

Now they were gone, killed by a little brat of a kid who was fast on the draw. Never mind they had miscalculated just how fast the kid was. They braced him, and in a gunfight one second could be the difference between life and death. Now they were dead and the kid had to pay for it.

Del Oldring put his glass down and pulled a pocket watch out of his vest and checked the time. He smiled, certain it was all over for the kid. By now he was swinging from a tree and Canfield, Fowler, and the new man, Cordell, would be back in their bunks at the Circle D Ranch.

That was one problem solved.

But there was the other one, the more personal one. This one went against his grain and ate at him more than anything else. It was tearing his insides out.

But it too, would be settled before the night was over. He would personally see to that. Del Oldring had a contact at the Emerald Hotel in town, a certain woman who cleaned rooms.

She had two children and her husband was in prison. He befriended her and comforted her. He gave her money when she needed a little extra cash. Sometimes he even gave her food such as smoked hams or canned fruit from the Circle D larder. On occasion he would spend the night at her little rundown cabin at the edge of town.

In his pocket he had the skeleton key that unlocked every room in the Emerald Hotel. All he needed now was a room number.

Oldring sat patiently toying with his whiskey glass, waiting. Just as he was about to check his watch again, a little boy came into the bar. He ran up to Oldring, whispered in his ear, and ran out before the bartender could react.

Oldring continued drinking for a few more minutes, and then he got up and walked over to the bar. As was his custom, he laid an eagle tip down for Frank, the bartender.

"Thanks, Mr. Oldring," Frank said. "Callin' it a night?"

"Yeah, Frankie," Oldring said. "Take it easy, fellah."

Oldring left. He walked down to the stables. He was met by old Ted, the attendant.

"Goin' home, Del?" Ted asked.

"Yeah, goin' home, Ted," the ramrod said. He yawned. "Gotta get up early."

Oldring mounted his horse and rode slowly up the street heading west for the Circle D, waving at the few people who turned to notice he was leaving town at this late hour. Once out of town and in the darkness, he turned to the north and nudged his horse into a stand of tall pine trees. He tied it there and continued on by foot. In a few minutes he was directly behind the Emerald Hotel.

He went quietly up on the porch and through the rear entrance to the lobby. The desk clerk was somewhere in the back, probably taking a nap. Oldring went quickly up the carpeted steps to the door of room six. He pulled out his boot knife, opened the door with the skeleton key, and went in.

Five minutes later he came slowly out, looked around, and went quietly down the stairs. In another ten minutes he was riding back to the Circle D. When he got there he saw that his boot knife was gone. He must have dropped it either in the pine stand or on the road.

12.

Nora Conroy stood on her porch in the warm early morning sunlight with a cup of coffee in her hand watching old Bern Langley send her cowboys out on range duty. The Bar C was a small spread so it didn't take very long. In a few moments all twelve cowboys were gone.

Bern walked over to the porch to see her.

"Good morning sleepy head," the old ramrod chuckled. When they were alone he treated her more like a daughter than an employer. He had been with the Bar C for fifteen years and was more of a father figure than a foreman.

"Good Morning, Bern," Nora said.

He knew that tone of voice. He heard it before, whenever something was bothering her.

"What's wrong?"

"He didn't come home last night from the Association meeting," Nora said.

Bern nodded. He didn't like seeing her this way. He always thought of her as a curly headed, freckle faced, happy little tomboy.

"Maybe he had an accident or somethin'," Bern said.

"Marshal Phelps would have sent someone out here, wouldn't he?"

Jilly Conroy came out wearing the dress she taught school in.

"Any word yet, momma?"

"No, dear."

"Well, I won't leave until we know what happened," Jilly insisted.

"I kin ride into town," Bern said. "Talk to the Marshal."

Nora nodded. "That might be the best thing to do."

"Alright, then," the old cowboy said.

Just as he turned to go to the corral, there was the sound of hoof beats behind the bunkhouse. In a few moments the kid, Sid, and Cordell came riding up and into the yard. Sid was slumped over in the saddle.

The kid and Cordell quickly dismounted and untied the wounded cowboy. Sid slid out of the saddle and Cordell grabbed him.

Nora gasped. "Bring him up here!"

The kid and Bern carried Sid up on the porch and set him down in a cedar chair. He looked pale and glassy-eyed.

"He's lost some blood," the kid said.

"I'm fine," Sid groaned. "I'm gonna ride."

"No you're not, Sid Turner," Nora said firmly. "Keep him there, boys. I'll go get the box."

Nora hurried into the house. Jilly stared at Sid.

"Hi, Miss Jilly," Sid said weakly, trying to smile.

"Hi, Sid," Jilly said in a sad tone. "You ain't gonna die, are you?"

"Heck, no," the kid cut in. "Nobody kin kill ol' Sid."

Jilly Conroy stared at the kid.

"You were here before," she said. "You're kid Breen, the killer, aren't you?" It was more of an accusation than a question. For a moment their eyes locked, staring boldly, neither one flinching.

The kid chuckled. "Yep, that's me. Killer Breen. You better watch out or I'll eat you up, little girl."

"Come on an' try it," Jilly sneered. "I ain't afraid of you, Kid Breen."

Nora came out of the house with the medicine box.

"Take his shirt off boys," she ordered. Bern and the kid helped Sid out of his jacket and shirt. Nora inspected the wound. The bullet barely nicked his shoulder bone and had gone clean through the muscle. "It ain't so bad, Sid. The bleeding has mostly stopped."

"Thet's good, "Sid said.

Nora poured some alcohol on a rag.

"This is gonna hurt Sid. You ready?"

"Sure, go ahead. I kin take it, ma'am." Sid said.

Nora swabbed the wound clean of blood. The cowboy clenched his teeth, groaning.

"Heck, thet weren't nothin'," Sid Turner said and fainted.

Old Bern chuckled. "Sid sure kin take it, can't he?"

"Poor Sid," Jilly said.

Nora finished cleaning the wound and started wrapping it. Cordell watched her closely. Jilly noticed.

"He's starin' at you, momma," Jilly said. "Bold as brass!" Then, to Cordell, "Why are you starin' at my momma, mister?"

"I'm counting the freckles on her pretty face," Cordell replied with a smile. "I've never seen a carrot top, blue eyed beauty like her before."

"What's your name, sir?" Nora said as she closed the medicine box. She stood up facing Cordell, inches from him. They stared into each other's eyes. There was a half-smile on her lips.

"Cordell, ma'am. Jack Cordell."

"Well, Mr. Cordell, I'm a married woman, in case you hadn't noticed."

"Married or not, ma'am, you are sure good to the eyes."

"He's a slick talking carpetbagger, momma." Jilly said.

Nora looked down at Sid. "Bring him in upstairs, boys." They put Sid's shirt back on him. Cordell picked him up and followed Nora into the house and upstairs to an empty bedroom. The others followed.

As they laid him on the bed he came to.

"Am I dead yet?" Sid asked dreamily.

"Yep," the kid chuckled. "Yer dead an' we're all ghosts."

"Are you able to eat, Sid?" Nora asked.

"Oh, sure," the wounded cowboy said. "You got any pie, ma'am?"

They all laughed.

"I think he'll be okay," Cordell said. He turned to Nora, "You sure did a nice job of fixing that bullet hole. Can you do the same for me, ma'am?"

He pulled open his jacket and pointed to his left side where his shirt was soaked with blood.

"I noticed that," Nora said. "Pull up your shirt, Mr. Cordell."

She inspected the wound. "It's only a graze, but it could get infected." She prepared another alcohol wipe and dabbed roughly at the wound. Cordell felt the heat and let out a gasp.

"Oh, I'm so sorry," Nora said, as if concerned. "Did I hurt you Mr. Cordell?"

"Oh no, ma'am, I'm just fine."

"Pull your shirt up higher and I'll wrap you up," Nora said.

In a few minutes she had a bandage around his waist. He tucked his shirt back in. After that they went down to the kitchen. Nora got up a breakfast of bacon, eggs, biscuits, and coffee for the kid and Cordell. Jilly took the same up to Sid.

As they sat around the table, Nora asked the kid, "Mind tellin' me what happened, Mr. Breen?"

"No, ma'am, I don't. It started when Mr. Cordell an' two Circle D cowboys come ta hang me an' kill Sid."

"Jesus!" Bern said.

"But Cordell kilt the two Circle D men instead."

"Where did all this happen?" Nora asked.

"At your north-end line shack, ma'am," Cordell said.

"Oh, oh! The cat's outta the bag," old Bern said.

"And what were you and Sid doing at the north-end line shack, Mr. Breen?" Nora asked.

"It's my fault, Nora," Bern said.

"I see. You let the two of them hide there?"

"Yes, ma'am."

"And Oldring found out?"

"Yes ma'am. I guess he's got spies everywhere."

Nora nodded and sighed. She took a sip of coffee and looked at the kid and Cordell. "You both will have to leave. Sid as well. I'm sorry. I hope you understand."

"I do ma'am," the kid said.

"Why can't they stay a while, momma?" Jilly asked. "Why not?"

"Because six Circle D cowboys have been killed. The men who killed them are right here in this house. Your father will not want them here when he comes home."

"Your mother is right," Cordell said. "We shouldn't be here. Oldring will find out. Innocent people might get hurt."

"If Oldring gets wind of who's here, he and his men will come down on us like the hammers of hell, Jilly," Bern said.

"I'm sorry," Nora said, looking down at her coffee cup.

"No deed to apologize, ma'am," Cordell said. "You have to protect your family. We understand that. Ah, do I get a goodbye kiss?"

They all laughed at the joke.

Suddenly they heard horses out on the road as they came into the yard and stopped.

"It's Oldring!" Jilly whispered.

"Everyone stay here," Cordell said. "If it's him, he'll want just me and the kid. Come on, kid."

Cordell and Kid Breen went out to the porch. They saw Marshal Phelps and his Deputy standing in the yard. When he saw them he looked surprised. It quickly changed to glaring anger.

"What the hell are you two doing out here?"

"It's a long story, Marshal," Cordell said.

"Where's Mrs. Conroy?"

"Here I am, Marshal!" Nora, Bern, and Jilly came out on the porch.

The Marshal took his hat off and looked down at the ground for a quick moment then looked up at Nora. "Can we talk, ma'am?"

For a moment Nora and Jilly stared at each other.

"Oh, no!" Jilly cried in surprise.

Nora went down the porch steps. She led the Marshal over to the fence and they faced each other.

"Give it to me straight, Marshal."

"Are you sure?"

"Yes."

"Your husband and Valerie Denton were found together in a room at the Emerald Hotel this morning," the Marshal said quietly. "They were murdered."

Nora looked away, searching for words to reply. All she could think of saying was, "Together?"

"Yes, Together."

"I see. Together." Nora turned back to the Marshal.

The Marshal nodded and looked across the yard to avoid seeing the hurt in Nora's eyes.

"Is there anything I can do, Mrs. Conroy? Should I have the body brought out today?" he said, turning back to her.

"No."

"Tomorrow?"

"No."

"Ah, when, then, ma'am?"

"Bury the son of a bitch in town, in the graveyard there," Nora said coldly. "I'll pay the bill."

"Are you sure? Do you need more time, Mrs. Conroy?"

"No, I don't need more time, Marshal."

"I'll find the killer, I promise."

"When you do, give him my warm regards, Marshal."

There was an awkward silence for a few moments. Nora and the Marshal walked back to the house. The Marshal and the Deputy mounted up.

"If you need anything, anything at all, Mrs. Conroy, please let me know."

"Thank you, Marshal."

Nora watched from the porch as Marshal Phelps and his Deputy rode slowly out to the road. They were soon out of sight around the bend.

"Jilly," Nora said. "Your stepfather is dead."

Jilly said, "Gosh! That's too bad, momma." She went into the house.

"I need to be alone awhile, Bern," Nora said.

"Sure, ma'am." Berm motioned and he, the kid, and Cordell walked down into the yard and over to the bunkhouse to smoke.

Nora Conroy stood on her porch in the warm morning sun staring out at the field of pine trees beyond her yard. At first she felt nothing and then it slowly came to her that she was a widow again. She had regrettably married a very handsome, overbearing man, a man who had dominated her for the last five years. Now, after two years of neglecting her, he died in the arms of another woman.

It was over and she didn't know how to react. For a moment Nora Conroy felt like a bird in a cage where someone had forgotten to close the door.

She could now fly free again.

13.

It was late morning. The kid and Cordell slept in the bunkhouse with the Bar C cowhands. Breakfast was over and the cowboys were all out on range duty. Sid was feeling better. He and the kid were talking to Jilly on the porch.

Cordell saw Nora behind the ranch house hanging out clothes. He left his horse in the yard and went over and stood watching her. He noticed how the sunlight danced along the edge of her short, deep red, wavy hair. He like the lines of her body in the men's clothing she wore. Whenever she smiled the freckles on her cheeks moved.

"You should be getting on your way, Mr. Cordell," Nora said. "Standing here watching me isn't good for your health, sir. Mr. Oldring will be looking for you."

"Well, now that I've seen heaven, I can die a happy man, ma'am," Cordell said.

"You have a smooth tongue, Mr. Cordell. My late husband had a smooth tongue, too."

Cordell came closer to Nora and looked down at her.

"You deserved better than him, ma'am. A decent man would have died before hurting you like he did."

"Bern has been talking too much."

"You're too good for any man around here."

"Doe that include you, too, Mr. Cordell?"

"It surely does, ma'am," Cordell said. "Especially me."

Nora turned to face Cordell, looking up at him.

"Who are you, Mr. Cordell? You go out to hang a man and you save his life instead and put your own at risk. Why?"

"Let's just say I have a code, ma'am. A man is no good without a code."

"Neither is a woman, Mr. Cordell."

They didn't say anything for a while, as if they had run out of words or were just trying to read each other's minds. Cordell wanted to reach out and touch her but he didn't.

"Where will you go?"

"To town to brace Oldring."

"Please don't. He'll kill you."

"No. He won't."

"I wish I could believe that. You don't know his reputation. He's very fast with a gun. So are his cowboys."

"Are you worried about me?"

"Perhaps. Maybe." She hesitated then said, "Yes."

"Why?"

"I don't know." She looked up at him. "I don't know, but I am."

"I'd like to stay around a while, when I come back."

"If you come back, you may," Nora said.

"I won't be able to stay a long time, just for a while."

"Alright. If you come back."

"I will."

She started to cry. "Please go, sir."

She turned her back to Cordell. He put his hand up and touched her hair with the tips of his fingers. She leaned back against him for a moment then pulled away.

"Goodbye." His voice was soft.

Cordell walked back to the yard to where the kid and Sid were flirting with Jilly on the porch.

"Kid," I'm leaving. It's best you stay here. You too, Sid. Just in case any of Oldring's men come payin' a visit."

"What, you runnin' out on us, Cordell?"

"I'm gonna settle with Oldring."

"He won't be alone."

"Yeah," Sid said. "He'll have at least three cowboys with him."

"I'm a going with you, Cordell," the kid said.

"If you wanna watch and learn, that's fine with me, Cordell said.

Bern came walking up from the bunkhouse.

"Bern," Cordell said. "I was just going to find you."

"Well, here I am? Whatta ya want?"

"I'd like you to go over to the Circle D and tell Oldring to meet me in town."

"You callin' Oldring out?" Bern said in surprise.

"That's right."

Old Bern whistled. "God almighty! I'm a goin'."

He quickly saddled up and left for the Circle D.

Sid said, "Heck! I might jest as well go too. I'm as crazy as the rest of you."

"Are you sure Sid," Cordell asked.

"Hell yes! I still got one good arm, the one I draw with."

"Well then, let's git mounted," the kid said. "I wanna be back here fer supper an' pie!"

"You are all crazy," Jilly said. She looked about to cry. She ran down the porch steps and around back to her mother.

In a few moments Sid, Cordell, and the kid were headed towards Barfield Springs at a slow ride.

"You sure you're feelin' alright, Sid?" the kid asked.

"Never felt better," Sid said.

"Yeah, well stay away from Jilly Conroy."

"Yeah? Why."

"Because I'm gonna marry her so she kin teach me readin' an' writin'."

"No you ain't," Sid chuckled. "She's gonna marry me."

"No she ain't!"

"Yes she is!"

"I'm a sayin' she ain't!"

"I'm a sayin' she is!"

It went like that all the way into town.

14.

The day after the double murder, a man riding into Barfield Springs found a boot knife on the side of the road about a mile from town. It had the initials D.O. carved in its wood handle. He took it to the Marshal to collect the twenty-five dollar reward. The Marshal warned him not to tell anyone and the man gave his word he wouldn't.

The Marshal put the knife on his desk. He and his deputy, Bob Leary, stood staring at it.

"Whatta we gonna do about this, Marshal?" Leary asked.

"I guess we gotta arrest Oldring, Bob."

Leary chuckled nervously. "Not me, Marshal. I got a wife, two kids, and a third on the way."

The deputy dropped his badge on the Marshal's desk and walked out of the jailhouse.

"Good luck, Marshal."

Marshal Phelps sighed as he sat down at his desk to roll a cigarette. Maybe Leary had the right idea. Phelps, too, had a wife and children. Who would take care of them if he was killed? Oldring wasn't going to give up without a fight. He usually had two or three cowboys with him. Especially his little clique of fast drawing men like Ned Fargo, Jude Danner, and Milt Renfrew.

No, maybe it was time to hang up the Marshal's badge here in Barfield Springs and find a more peaceful place to work. The town didn't pay enough for this twenty-four hour a day job. The Marshal was not only responsible for keeping the peace and arresting lawbreakers, he had to arrest drunks, settle arguments, jail vagrants and drifters, enforce town ordinances, and put the town to bed at night.

He also had to attend town meeting and give a town status report and he and his family were expected to be seen in church each Sunday. At the town meetings he usually got a lecture and a tongue-lashing for not doing this or not doing that. And he was to make sure his deputy cleaned up the streets and alleyways like a janitor, scooping up horse and dog droppings so that the townsfolk didn't step in it. If anyone stepped into horse poop, the Marshal was sure to hear about it.

Phelps had once been a cowboy. He was good with horses and was a fast draw. But when he met a girl and got married, he stopped riding the range and took a job as a deputy in town. After four years he got the Marshal's position. But now it looked like the end of the line.

Suddenly the Marshal's thoughts were interrupted by outside sounds. He walked slowly to the door and looked up the street and saw Jack Cordell, the kid from Del Rio, and Sid Turner, riding down the street past the Lusty Lady Saloon, toward the jailhouse.

One of Oldring's men came out of the saloon to watch as the three men came up to the jailhouse, dismounted, and went in.

Sid saw a boot knife on the Marshal's desk. "I know thet knife," Sid said. "It's Oldring's."

"It's got blood on it," the kid said.

"Yeah, he killed Mrs. Denton and Larry Conroy," the Marshal said.

"How come you ain't arrested him, Marshal," the kid asked.

"I'm callin' in the County Sheriff," the Marshal said. He didn't sound very confident.

"Why don't you arrest him now and send him on to the county seat for trial?" Cordell said.

"I can't. My deputy quit. Just walked out on me."

Cordell saw the deputy badge on the desk. He picked it up and looked it over.

"You got more of these?"

"Yeah, why?"

Cordell pinned on the deputy badge. "We'll need two more."

"It ain't legal unless I swear you in," the Marshal said.

Suddenly they heard voices out on the street.

"Hey, Marshal! It's me! Ned Fargo!"

The Marshal froze. He looked about to panic. Finally he settled his nerves.

"Whatta ya want, Fargo?"

"You got somethin' that belongs to Oldring," Fargo yelled. "He wants it back." Fargo paused for a moment.

"And Oldring says ta send them three ass holes out or we'll come in an' get 'em! You got that?"

The Marshal seemed cornered. He stared at Cordell.

"You'll have to go. I'm sorry. I got a family. Get out!"

"There's a better option, Marshal," Cordell said.

"What's that?"

"You deputize the three of us and we all go out there and kick Oldring's ass together. Otherwise you'd best bolt the door and hunker down for a long fight. We won't be leaving."

"You son of a bitch!" the Marshal said through clenched teeth. "Yer getting' me killed alongside the rest of you fools!"

"If he kills us, you're next because you know he killed Denton's wife. He's got to get his knife back and shut you up," Cordell said.

The Marshal thought a moment and then realized he was a dead man, one way, or the other.

"Hell, why not? Let's give them a real show, men!"

The Marshal got two deputy badges from his desk and pinned them on Sid and the kid.

"Raise yer right hands, you dumb sons-a-bitches!" the Marshal growled. "Under the powers granted me by the City Council of Barfield Springs, I hereby make you deputies."

"Whoopee I'm a deputy!" Sid hollered.

The Marshal chuckled. "At least for ten minutes. You'll all be pushing up daisies by then."

They all checked their guns for full loads.

"You any good, Marshal?" the kid asked.

"We'll soon see, kid." He looked at them and smiled. "Hell, let get this dance started."

The Marshal was the first out the door of the jailhouse. He stood on the porch looking up the road toward the Lucky Lady Saloon. Oldring, Fargo, Danner, and Renfrew were out in front, waiting. When they saw him they walked slowly onto the road and spread out, side-by-side. Fargo was on Oldring's right and Danner and Refrew were aligned on his left.

They came walking slowly towards the jail. The people who saw them either stopped to stare or ran for cover.

Cordell, Sid, and the kid came out on the porch. They stopped to look and then went out into the street. Cordell glanced at the Marshal who seemed glued to his spot.

"You joining the party, or not, Marshal?"

The Marshal inhaled deeply. He nodded.

"I'm in." He stepped out into the road next to Sid.

"Wait for them," Cordell said. "Don't rush it."

As it was, the kid was facing Ned Fargo, Cordell was facing Oldring, Sid was facing Danner, and the Marshal was facing Renfrew.

"Whose yers, Sid?" the kid asked.

"Danner. He's an ass-kisser." Sid sneered.

The kid chuckled. "Is he fast?"

"Oh, yeah. Very fast," Sid said.

"Then good-luck, pard," the kid said.

Ed Farnsworth, who owned the Barfield Springs Gazette, came out on his porch to look. He rubbed his eyes, thinking this wasn't real then realized it was.

"Oh, my God!" Farnsworth said. The others inside came out to look, too. "Get the presses ready, everybody! This is going to be big!"

Oldring and his men halted about forty feet from the jailhouse. He looked down at Cordell and sneered.

"Well, well, I've been looking for you Cordell, you back stabbing son of a bitch! I told you what I'd do to you if you crossed me. Remember what I said I'd do to you?"

"Yeah. You said you'd put a bullet between my eyes, Oldring," Cordell said calmly. "Well, here's your chance."

"Delmer Oldring," the Marshal cut in, "you are hereby under arrest for the cold blooded murder of Valerie Denton and Larry Conroy. Drop you gun and surrender to the law. If you don't I will have to take you by force."

Oldring, Fargo, Danner, and Renfrew looked at each other for a moment and burst out laughing.

"In a pig's ass, you will!" Oldring yelled. "Yer all gonna die!"

Oldring drew and a split second later his three gunnies slapped leather too.

The sound of eight guns blasting at once sounded like a cannon fusillade. Window vibrated along the street. Bystanders ducked and held their ears. Some ran and hid.

Ned Fargo, who was facing the kid, drew confidently with a smile. His gun was halfway out when the kid's Colt barked. The kid's shot slammed into his chest knocking him flat on his back.

Next to Fargo, Del Oldring made his move on Cordell.

"Die, you son of a bitch," Oldring screamed and drew.

Oldring was a bit late but he got off his shot. Cordell had shifted to one side and went into a crouch. Oldring's bullet cut a hole in his holster. Oldring didn't realize that he was already shot between the eyes. The big man's head snapped back on his neck and his legs turned to sand as he collapsed on his face in the street.

Cordell noticed that Sid was down, holding his side, and Danner was turning his gun on the kid. Cordell shot him in the heart before he could squeeze a shot off.

Renfrew, who had beat the Marshal by a second, shot at his head. His aim was too high and took the Marshal's hat off. The Marshal put two shots in Renfrew's chest, dropping him like a rock.

It all happened in less than a minute. The sounds of the gunshots echoed out beyond the town for a long time. Then a deep quiet settled in.

The kid rushed to Sid's side. He got down and cradled him in his arms.

"Shit," Sid said. He coughed up blood. He had been hit just below the heart. "I always knew Danner was faster than me."

"But you got him, partner," the kid said, his voice cracking. "You sure did."

"I did? No kiddin'?"

"No kiddin'. You plugged him dead center, Sid."

"Gosh. Ain't that somethin'." The light in Sid's eyes went out and he sighed. His body went limp in the kid's arms.

"So long, Sid," the kid said. His eyes flooded. He looked up at the crowd that gathered. "We was partners."

A young girl nearby began to cry.

The man from the Barfield Springs Gazette went into the newspaper office and began furiously writing down what he just witnessed.

15.

The next day an article appeared on the front page of the Barfield Springs Gazette that read:

"The reign of terror is over! The hold that Delmer Oldring and his notorious Circle D men had on the town of Barfield Springs was broken yesterday when Oldring and his three gunnies, Ned Fargo, Jude Danner, and Milton Renfrew were shot down by Marshal Phelps and three citizen volunteer deputies, one of whom was killed in the deadly shoot out."

The article went on in great detail giving a blow-by-blow description of the historic gun battle and the names of everyone involved. It gave as the reason for Oldring's arrest the fact that the Marshal possessed evidence that Oldring murdered the wife of his employer, Valerie Denton, in cold blood. It made no mention of Larry Conroy.

The owner of the Barfield Springs Gazette was a friend of Nora Conroy and was known for being sensitive and discrete. A later article mentioned Larry Conroy died of pneumonia

A week after the shootout Barfield Springs became a curiosity. People from all around the territory who heard about it came to see where it had taken place. The Marshal became a celebrity. His deputy returned and became the tour guide pointing out where the brave Marshal Phelps had faced down the vicious Oldring gang.

Out at the Circle D, George Denton decided he had enough of being a rancher in a wheel chair. Unable to ride and enjoy the outdoors, he put the ranch up for sale and went back east. His big ranch was parceled off into three sections and were quickly sold. The Circle D Ranch went out of existence. The cowhands went looking for work.

Things went on as usual at the Bar C except that the kid was hired on as Bern's second in command. He did this to be near Jilly. Nora relaxed her rules and let the two go to barn dances and picnics now and then. The kid's reputation as a gunfighter was a comfort to her, knowing it was there to protect the spread.

As for Nora, cowboys and ranchers came to court this newly made widow, this redheaded, freckled-face woman of the west. A woman who wore no makeup and smelled of fresh air and sage. They lined up at her door like ducks.

But she turned each and every one away and busied herself with chores at the ranch, cooking for the cowboys, mending their clothes, attending to their cuts and bruises, and cooking their favorite pies.

Some of the ranch hands went to Sunday church with her and Jilly.

One day, old Bern watched Nora as she stood on the porch staring out at the horizon.

"Where did he go, Bern?"

"He said you needed some grazin' room. He didn't want ta crowd ya, missy."

"He wasn't hurt, was he?"

"Not as I know of."

"He didn't even say goodbye."

"Fer some people goodbyes hurt too much," Bern said. "Then agin, if he didn't say goodbye then it ain't goodbye time yet. Anyway, I seen the way he eyeballed ya."

Nora chuckled. "You romantic old coot! You're just imagining things."

"Well, you better marry somebody or you'll be wearin' the porch down," Bern said.

"No, old friend, I'm done with marrying."

The old ramrod nodded and went down towards the barn. Nora went into the house.

The next day she got up early as usual and cooked breakfast for the cowhands. They got their orders from Bern and left. The kid got out the buckboard and took Jilly over to the schoolhouse. By mid-afternoon when everyone was gone, Nora did the wash and took it behind the house to hang it up to dry.

She was lost in thought and never heard the horse come up and stop a few yards behind her.

"Did anyone ever tell you how beautiful you look with the sun in your hair, ma'am?"

Nora knew the voice but didn't turn.

"Did anyone tell you that you're a smooth talker, Mr. Cordell?"

"I think you did, ma'am, once."

Cordell dismounted and walked slowly over to Nora. She turned to face him. He stared down into her eyes

"You ran off. Why?" she asked.

"I did some killing and had to get it out of my mind," Cordell said. "I wouldn't have been much fun to be around."

"Is it always like that, afterwards?"

"Yes. Mostly. I have to reorder my thinking, stay drunk for days. I don't take killing men lightly."

"Out here, in the west, it's a part of our lives, isn't it?" Nora said. She touched his face gently with the fingers of one hand. "I was worried about you. I thought you would be killed."

He took the hand and kissed it.

"I can't stay long, Nora."

"It doesn't matter. A day, a week, a month, a year."

"However long I stay, I'll treat every day with you as a gift from God and be grateful for it."

"Promise one thing?"

"What?"

"You won't ride off again like that without saying goodbye first?"

"I promise. I swear."

Suddenly old Bern came running up, panting heavily. When he saw Cordell he smiled.

"You got here jest in time, Cordell!"

"What's wrong, Bern?" Nora asked.

"I got two mares droppin' foals at the same time! If it don't rain it pours, gosh dang it all!"

Cordell and Nora laughed.

"Well, then, let's go!"

Cordell took Nora's hand. They followed old Bern down to the Barn.

He jabbered all the way.

The End.

About the Author

R. Annan is a seasoned and traveled author with many interests. As a career serviceman he served in Korea and Vietnam. He also completed a one-year course at the Defense Language Institute at Monterey, California, and graduated from the University of South Florida with a B.A. in Art and Art History. After taking a two-year course in screenwriting at the Hollywood Scriptwriting Institute, he established The Old Time Radio Club Time Machine as both a scriptwriter and an actor.

A Note from the Author

Thank you for reading my book. If you enjoyed it, would you please consider rating and reviewing it? I'd enjoy your feedback. Here's a link to my author's page on Amazon: www.amazon.com/author/rannan

Look for other books to appear soon. Thank you!

www.ingramcontent.com/pod-product-compliance
Lightning Source LLC
Chambersburg PA
CBHW060643130626
46555CB00002B/935